Where Mermaids Live

LINDA L. BRIGHTBILL

This is a work of fiction. All of the characters, names, incidents, organizations, and dialogue in this novel are either the products of the author's imagination or are used fictitiously.

Archway Publishing books may be ordered through booksellers or by contacting:

Archway Publishing
1663 Liberty Drive
Bloomington, IN 47403
www.archwaypublishing.com
844-669-3957

Interior Image Credit: Gabriel Middleton

ISBN: 978-1-6657-0648-3 (sc)
ISBN: 978-1-6657-0650-6 (hc)
ISBN: 978-1-6657-0649-0 (e)

Print information available on the last page.

Archway Publishing rev. date: 04/24/2021

This book is dedicated to
my grandchildren.

May they always carry a child
like spirit in their hearts.

Acknowledgements

The author wishes to acknowledge and thank Gabriel Middleton for his amazing illustrations and vision.

The idea of this book came to me after one day sitting on the beach. A grandmother and her granddaughter walking by, stopped to look at some rocks embedded in the sand. The granddaughter looked inside the rocks and turned to her grandmother with a puzzled look. Her grandmother looked at her and said. "That is where mermaids live." The little girl smiled, looked inside again, took her grandmothers hand and they continued on their way. That vision of the little girl has always stayed with me, hence Where Mermaids Live was put into pictures and words."

Always......

Always Dream more,
Always Give more,
And most of all,
Always Love More.

Mermaids live beneath the sea in the bluest waters you have ever seen.

They live in Castles built of the finest white sand, adorned with the most perfect of sea shells found in their land.

Their hair is long and flows with the currents of the sea, shining in every color of the rainbow as far as the eye can see.

They wear jewelry made of gems and pirates gold, found in ships lost in days of old.

Their song is sweet and clear, when you listen closely enough, you will hear it travel through the waves and air.

They have the most beautiful tails
and you may see, how they swim
with the dolphins in the sea.

How do I know these things you may wonder? Because you see, one of those Mermaids is me!

About the Author

Linda L. Brightbill was born and raised in Harrisburg, Pennsylvania, where she still lives. She is the mother of three children and grandmother of four.

CPSIA information can be obtained
at www.ICGtesting.com
Printed in the USA
BVHW021949070921
616247BV00025B/365

9 781665 706483